IFEOMA ONYEFULU was born and brought up in eastern Nigeria. After studying business management in London, she trained as a photographer. *A is for Africa*, her first book for Frances Lincoln, was described by Books for Keeps as "stepping from a darkened room straight into noon sunshine". It was chosen by Child Education as one of the best information books of 1993, and was nominated for the 1994 Kate Greenaway Medal. It was followed by *Emeka's Gift – An African Counting Story* and *One Big Family – Sharing Life in an African Village*. Ifeoma lives in London with her husband and two young sons.

To Chika and Chukwudi,
for allowing me into their world

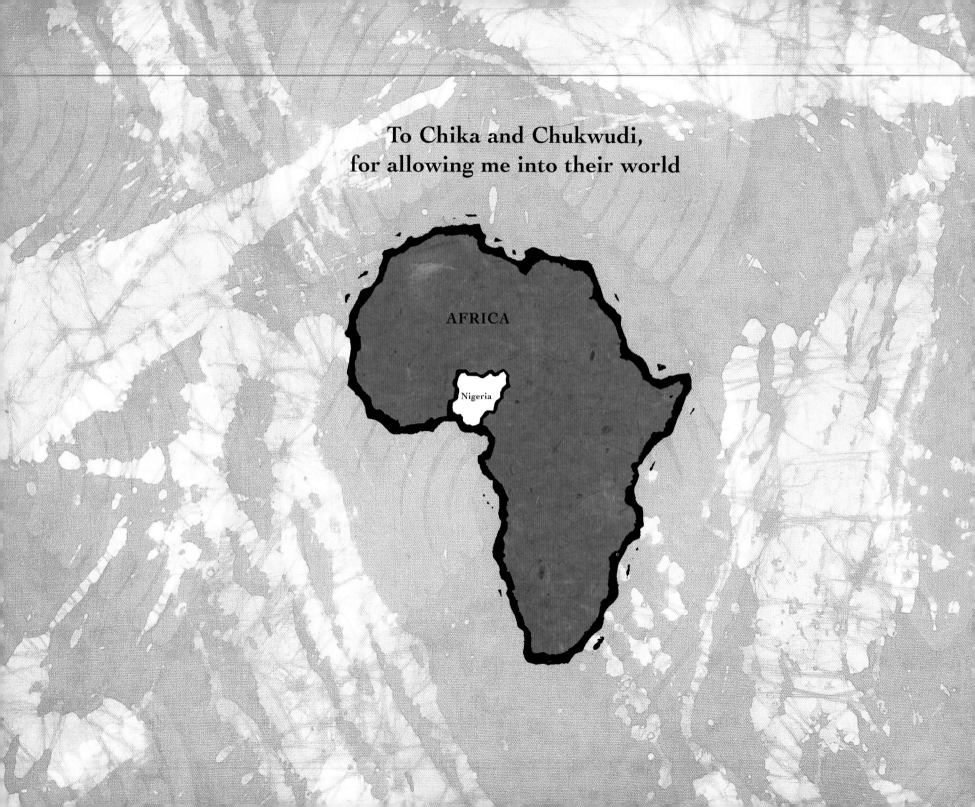

AFRICA

Nigeria

Chidi Only Likes Blue

Ifeoma Onyefulu

F

FRANCES LINCOLN

CHILDREN'S BOOKS

 My name is Nneka. (pronounced n-EK-a). My little brother's name is Chidi (CHEE-dee). We often play together, and whenever we play the game Colours, Chidi says, "Nneka, my favourite colour is blue. That is the best colour in the whole world."

Then I ask, "Why do you always say blue?"

And he says, "Because the sky is blue, and my best shirt is blue."

"Perhaps Chidi does not know the names of any other colours," says Mother.

So, Chidi, here are the names of the other colours I know, and why I like them.

 I like red because Great-Uncle wears a special red cap. Only the chiefs chosen by our king or *igwe* (ee-gweh) are allowed to wear these caps. The chiefs are older and wiser than everyone else in the village and they help the igwe make important decisions.

Great-Uncle wears his red cap whenever he goes to ceremonies and meetings. Here he is, with two other chiefs.

 I like yellow because it is the colour of *gari* (GAH-ree). Gari is made from cassava roots, which are cleaned, grated, soaked and then fried in palm oil. Last of all, they are mixed with boiling water to be eaten with soup.

Here, the gari grains have been piled up in bowls to be sold by the roadside.

 Uncle John uses green leaves from palm trees to build roofs on houses. Here he is, making a shelter to store his yams away from the hot sunshine.

Mother's friend, Mrs Okoli, uses green leaves from a plant called *akwukwo uma* (ar-KWOO-KWO U-ma) to wrap up foods like *moi-moi* (moy-moy) before they are cooked in the pot. Moi-moi is made from beans, and the leaves give it a delicious taste – though they look much darker when cooked.

Black is the colour people in my village use to decorate their houses during the dry season. Usually men build the houses and women paint the walls black with *uli* (oo-lee). Uli is a juice made from the seeds of the uli tree.

The women's fingers move fast across the walls like spiders when they are painting, because they must finish their drawings before the uli dries up.

Children sometimes paint the walls, too.

White is the colour of the chalks grown-ups use to make wishes for long life or for children. The chalk is cut out of the ground and then made into different shapes and sizes.

Here is some chalk that Grandfather placed on the floor yesterday, when his friends came to see him. One of them, Chief Nduka (N-doh-ka), picked up a piece and drew lines on the floor.

"Chief Nduka has just made a wish," Grandfather said to me. "Women make wishes too, but in a different way. When a woman makes a wish, she picks up the chalk and rubs it on her belly. Wishes are prayers said silently."

I like pink. It is the colour of the flowers that grow around our house. I always put some in my hair when we play Princes and Princesses.

 Cream is the colour of the gourds that Grandmother uses. They grow from creepers, and she cuts them in half, cleans them and stores palm-nut oils and soaps in them.

Cream also makes me think of the chewing sticks my sister Ebele (eh-beh-leh) uses to brush her teeth. The sticks are cleaned and cut into small pieces. When Ebele chews one, it softens until it is like a brush. Here she is, cleaning her teeth.

I like brown. Grandmother keeps two brown wooden stools in her kitchen. She sits on one while she is cooking, and I sit on the other when I am helping her.

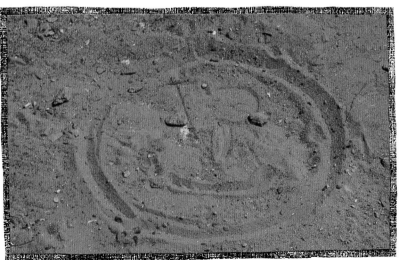

Brown is the colour of the sand around our house. I like to draw pictures in it.

Here is a brown wooden board my friends use to play a game called *okwe* (OH-kway). The board has fourteen hollows carved into it, and the game is played with seeds.

Father is going to teach me to play okwe. He says it will help me count properly.

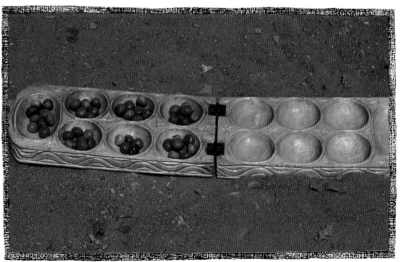

 I like the gold necklaces Mother wears on special occasions. They make her look as pretty as the sunshine.

Mother has made me a beautiful dress of all the colours I like. She says I have been a good teacher to Chidi. But Chidi still likes blue best of all!

Textile design for endpapers by Chinye Onyefulu

OTHER PICTURE BOOKS IN PAPERBACK
FROM FRANCES LINCOLN

Welcome Dede!
Ifeoma Onyefulu

Amarlai has a new baby cousin and he can't wait for her to be given a name:
a traditional African name will tell people where she comes from and which child
she is in the family. When the naming day arrives a special ceremony is held with
blessings, gifts and feasting. Everyone is happy and Amarlai is happiest of all:
his baby cousin now has a name – Dede!

The Leopard's Drum
Jessica Souhami

How a very small tortoise outwits a boastful leopard to capture his drum
is dramatically retold in this traditional tale from West Africa.
Jessica has adapted shadow puppet images to create her bold illustrations.

Chinye
Obi Onyefulu
Illustrated by Evie Safarewicz

Poor Chinye! Back and forth through the forest she goes, fetching and carrying
for her cruel stepmother. But strange powers are watching over her, and soon
her life will be magically transformed… An enchanting retelling of a traditional
West African folk tale of goodness, greed and a treasure-house of gold.

Frances Lincoln titles are available from all good bookshops.
You can also buy books and find out more about your favourite titles,
authors and illustrators on our website: www.franceslincoln.com